DISNEP

# The ARISTOKITTENS

# Welcome to the Creature Café

Printed in the United States of America

First Paperback Edition, April 2022

First Hardcover Edition, April 2022

1 3 5 7 9 10 8 6 4 2

ISBN 978-1-368-06576-4 (Paperback), ISBN 978-1-368-06972-4 (Hardcover)

FAC-020093-22063

Library of Congress Control Number: 2021946263

Book design by Catalina Castro

Visit disneybooks.com

DISNEY

The
ARISTOKITTENS

# Welcome to the Creature Café

## By Jennifer Castle

### Illustrated by Sydney Hanson

DISNEP PRESS

Los Angeles • New York

# Chapter 1

On a bright, warm morning in Paris, inside a grand mansion on a cobblestone street, three kittens sat looking up at a big wooden door. Their tails swished nervously back and forth.

"Maybe we shouldn't go in today," said one, a white kitten named Marie. "Mama told us to go play in the courtyard."

"But that's *so* boring," said her brother, a gray kitten named Berlioz.

He tapped the door with one tiny claw. "We're going to have a lot more fun in there."

"Yeah, we can't just go back to our same old routine," added orange kitten Toulouse, the other brother. "Not after everything that's happened!"

The three kittens, along with their mother, Duchess, had just experienced the adventure of their lives. Maybe even all *nine* of their lives. They'd been catnapped by a scheming butler, but with courage, luck, and some critter cooperation, they'd found their way home to their beloved human, Madame Adelaide Bonfamille. Along the way, they'd seen many amazing things and met fascinating new friends . . . especially some very cool alley cats.

Marie smiled. "You're right. Let's do it. On my count! One . . . two . . ."

Before she could say *three*, Toulouse pushed open the door himself and burst into the room.

"Typical," Marie sighed. "But yay! We're in!"

Ever since Madame had opened up her home as a shelter for the stray kitties of Paris, felines of every type imaginable had filled the parlor behind the big door: busy and lazy, chunky and fluffy, fancy and scruffy. The kittens liked to call it Alley Cat Parlor.

Berlioz raced past twin tabbies snoring in their bunk beds and a group of four alley cats playing cards, straight to the piano. He leapt onto the keys, causing a sound like pots and pans crashing to the floor.

"*Mrow!*" one of the alley cats exclaimed, flattening his ears.

"Sorry!" Berlioz replied. "I just can't wait to play the new song I wrote!"

Toulouse rushed to the far corner, where an easel, an empty canvas, and painting supplies were set up. He dipped one paw into the yellow paint and one into the black, then smeared both blobs of color onto the canvas.

"A masterpiece!" declared a little gray mouse who was standing nearby, munching on a cracker.

"Hello, Roquefort!" Toulouse said. "Do you really like my painting?"

Roquefort, who lived in the walls of the mansion, was a loyal friend to the kittens and their mama. He'd helped rescue them when they were catnapped.

Now he liked to hang around Alley Cat Parlor, nibbling on leftovers and licking the milk bowls clean.

"I love it!" Roquefort exclaimed. "It's a delicious banana, right? No, wait. A yellow cupcake with chocolate icing?"

Toulouse frowned. "It's a *bumblebee*."

"Oh," Roquefort said with a disappointed sigh. "Well, that's not yummy at all."

Marie bounded past her brothers and through the door that led to the kitchen, where a fluffy gray cat sat on the counter, kneading dough with his two front paws.

"Louis!" Marie said, laughing. "You're covered in flour!"

"Oh, my!" the cat said. He shook out

his fur, and the flour rose up around him like a cloud. Now he appeared to be the fluffy *black* cat he really was. "Would you like to help me make kitty croissants?"

"Yes, please! Your pastries are the best things I've ever tasted, Louis. Do you think I could be a chef like you someday?"

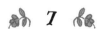

"*Ahem-meow,*" said a voice behind Marie. "That all depends on what your mother does when she catches you down here."

Marie spun around to see a big orange-and-white tomcat grinning whisker to whisker. It was Thomas O'Malley, the coolest of the cool cats, who'd helped their family during the big catnapping adventure. He'd since become their stepfather.

"*Toulouse! Marie! Berlioz!*" Duchess called from upstairs. "Come along, darlings! Madame is taking us to the park!"

Marie shot a panicked look at Louis and O'Malley, then rushed back into the parlor to warn her brothers. "It's Mama! Quick! Hide!"

Berlioz and Toulouse both tried to scurry under the same chair, causing a kitten collision.

"Ow!" Berlioz howled, swatting at his brother. "Can you be more careful?"

"Hey, *you* crashed into *me*!" Toulouse said, swatting back.

Marie skidded across the floor, then hopped into a basket kitty bed. She dove under a blanket just as Duchess, an elegant white cat in a sparkly gold collar, walked into the room.

"Duchess!" O'Malley said as he strutted through the kitchen door and spotted the kittens' mama. "Can I just tell you how much your eyes still sparkle like sapphires?"

Duchess blinked her big blue eyes slowly at O'Malley. Once, twice, three times. Then she glanced around the room, noticing the lumpy blanket in the basket.

"Thank you, Thomas, darling," Duchess said. Then she smiled sweetly. "Now, can *you* tell our kittens to come out of their hiding places and meet me outside?"

Duchess, O'Malley, and the kittens strolled along behind Madame into the Luxembourg Gardens, one of Paris's busiest parks.

"Mama," Berlioz asked Duchess, "are you angry that we've been spending so much time with the alley cats?"

Duchess nuzzled Berlioz's cheek with hers. "I'm not mad, my darlings, but you must promise not to keep things from me anymore. It's a kitten's job to be curious, but not secretive."

"We promise!" the kittens meowed, weaving in and out of Duchess's legs.

Duchess laughed. "Very good. Now, go play while Thomas and I help Madame find the perfect picnic spot."

Marie, Berlioz, and Toulouse raced onto the grass. They loved the park! It was filled with so many colorful sights, exciting sounds, and interesting smells. Nearby, two children tossed a small rubber ball back and forth. Berlioz started watching, then Toulouse joined in, and soon all three kittens were hypnotized by the ball as it flew through the air.

Suddenly, *PONK!* One of the

children threw the ball too hard. It bounced off a tree, fell to the pavement, and rolled away.

"Let's catch it!" Toulouse shouted as he launched himself like a rocket after the ball.

"Wait up!" Marie called, taking off behind him.

Now Berlioz was chasing the ball, too, and it picked up speed as it rolled toward the park gates.

*"Chook-chook-chook!"* a voice chattered from above. A brown squirrel with a big bushy tail perched on a tree branch, watching the kittens. "Where are you going? Why are you running? What is happening?"

"Hi, Pouf!" Toulouse called to the

squirrel. "Can't talk now! Important kitten business!"

Berlioz, Toulouse, and Marie pursued the ball as it traveled across the street, around a corner, and into an alley. There, it bounced off a wall and flew back toward them.

Marie jumped for it but missed. Berlioz leapt next, but he missed, too, and landed on Marie. Toulouse made a final grab for the ball, but it escaped his paws as he fell onto the kitten pile.

"*Ow!*" they all yowled.

The ball was headed straight for a metal grate in the wall . . . when a tiny door in the grate opened! A rat scampered out. The kittens

watched the ball sail through the door
and disappear.

"Um . . ." Berlioz said. "What just
happened?"

"Should we go after it?" Marie
asked.

"Mama *did* say it was our job to be
curious," Toulouse replied.

The kittens inched toward the open door and, one by one, crept through.

They tumbled down a couple steps and landed landing in a dark space. Toulouse and Berlioz flattened their ears and puffed up their tails, but Marie just sniffed the air. Light glowed from around a corner.

"You go first," Berlioz said to Toulouse.

Toulouse sprang forward, but then he froze, glancing back nervously at his siblings. "It's not like I'm afraid, but I . . . um . . ."

"Oh. Meow. Gosh," Marie said. "*I'll* go first. Follow me."

Slowly, stepping softly on their paws, the kittens slinked around the corner.

They gasped at what they saw.

An empty restaurant. More than empty. Old and abandoned, with dust everywhere. Some of the wooden tables and chairs were broken. Windows were cloudy from dirt, and a rickety piano stood against a far wall.

"Is this some old café?" Berlioz asked. He walked over to the piano and played some notes, but they rang out horribly off-key.

"I think so, but something's not quite right," Toulouse said. "What is it?"

Marie thought for a moment, her whiskers twitching, and then exclaimed: "It's small! Everything's *our* size!"

Toulouse's face brightened as he bounded through the room. "You're

right! I bet you—*pffft . . . pffft . . .* Yuck, I
just ran through a cobweb!"

Marie and Berlioz started laughing
at their brother. But then:

*"GRRR . . . WOOF!"*

The kittens jumped, their fur
standing on end.

*"GRRR . . . WOOF! WOOF! WOOF!"*

An angry French bulldog stood
behind them, baring his teeth.

# Chapter 2

The kittens huddled together, flattening their ears.

The French bulldog growled again and took a step closer. He had light brown fur and a white chest.

"I've got this," Toulouse whispered as he moved protectively in front of his littermates. He then arched his back and fluffed up his tail, trying to make himself look much, much bigger. "*Mrrrow! Ffft-ffft-ffft-ffft.* Go away and leave us alone!"

Toulouse held up a paw, showing his tiny claws, and swiped at the air.

The bulldog froze in his tracks. His eyes grew wide.

"He's frightened!" Marie whispered to Berlioz. "Maybe Toulouse has actually gotten much scarier!"

The dog burst out laughing.

He laughed so hard he flopped onto the ground, his tongue hanging out of his mouth.

Toulouse flattened his ears and tilted his head, looking confused. Marie took a deep breath and inched closer to the dog.

"What are you doing, Marie?" Berlioz called softly after her. "You could get hurt!"

Marie looked back at her brother and said, "Mama always tells us, 'Good manners and kindness are always in fashion.'"

"Yeah," Berlioz said, "but . . . I don't think that bulldog cares about what's in fashion."

Marie kept approaching the dog, her whiskers quivering with fear. She'd almost reached him when he stopped laughing and suddenly sat up straight. She took a deep breath, gathered all her courage, and smiled her friendliest smile.

"G-good afternoon, monsieur. My n-n-name is Marie. Charmed to make your acquaintance."

She held out a dainty paw.

The bulldog stared at the paw.

"Is it just me," Berlioz whispered to his brother, "or does he look hungry?"

The bulldog sat up extra straight

and . . . broke into a huge grin. He held
out his own paw, touching it to Marie's.

"Bonjour, Marie," he said in a gruff
but polite voice. "My name is Pierre."
Marie looked over her shoulder at
Berlioz and Toulouse. Her expression
said, *I told you so!*

"I sure do hate it when she's right," Toulouse murmured.

"These are my brothers, Toulouse and Berlioz," Marie told the bulldog. "I'm sure Toulouse is very sorry that he hissed and swatted at you like that. We were just frightened."

"Oh, no harm done," Pierre said. "I was scared, too. Apologies for all the barking and snarling. I often find rats here playing cards and eating the furniture, so that's how I chase them away. When I got closer, I realized you were kittens!"

"Is this where you live?" Toulouse asked.

"Bah, no!" Pierre replied. "Perhaps you've seen the Luxembourg Brasserie restaurant across from the park? My humans are the owners. I live with them in the apartment right above."

"We *have* seen the Luxembourg Brasserie!" Marie exclaimed. "Every time we walk by, our stepfather, Thomas, says those are his favorite smells in the whole world."

"So what is this?" Toulouse asked. "Is it part of the restaurant?"

Pierre let out a sigh and started walking around the room. With his nose, he pushed a fallen chair back into place.

"This was a separate restaurant," Pierre said softly. "Le Café des Creatures. Or as we all knew it, the Creature Café."

*"Humans,"* Berlioz said, shaking his head. "Where do they come up with these names?"

"This wasn't a human restaurant,"

Pierre said with a knowing smile. "It was a restaurant for animals. All the animals of Paris, in fact! Whether you had fur or feathers or scales, if you had a tail or no tail . . . everyone was welcome. Even the rats—as long as they behaved themselves."

Marie looked around at the broken chairs and tables and the old piano in the corner. "Oh, it must have been just super."

Pierre sighed, then ran a paw along a dusty tabletop. "It really was. Always filled with music and delicious food and excellent company."

"Well, now it's a super *mess*," Toulouse said.

"Toulouse!" Marie scolded, swatting her brother. "That's rude!"

"Not rude at all," Pierre said. "It is a mess. Bah! My dear friend Monsieur Midnight would be so sad to see his beautiful restaurant like this. He was the best feline chef in all of Paris, and he was always so proud of the café. My job was to bring him leftovers from the restaurant upstairs, and—voilà!—like magic, he would turn them into the most amazing dishes."

"Where is Monsieur Midnight now?" Toulouse asked.

"Oh, I'm sure he's living a fabulous life in America with his human," Pierre replied. "Midnight's human and my human are brothers, you see, and together they ran the restaurant upstairs. But the brothers had a big fight, and then Midnight and I had a fight over *their* fight. When his human left for New York City, Midnight went with him."

Tears formed in Pierre's eyes, and he dabbed at them with a paw.

"Oh, no," Toulouse whispered to Marie and Berlioz. "I didn't mean to make him so upset."

"How can we cheer him up?" Marie asked.

"We could sing a song," Berlioz suggested. "The one that always cheers up Mama when she's feeling down."

"That's a great idea!" Marie said.

"Not *that* song," Toulouse groaned, rolling his eyes. "You both sing it so loud."

Marie stuck out her tongue at Toulouse. "Well, it's two against one."

She turned to Pierre. "Monsieur Pierre, we have a little something to help you feel better. A one, a two, and a one-two-three."

Berlioz sat down and started thumping one front paw against the floor, creating a beat. Then he and Marie began to sing:

*When the world makes your fur stand*
*    on end*
*When you feel like you need a forever*
*    friend*

Toulouse let out a sigh, then joined in, too.

*Just call my name and flick your tail*
*I'll come running, without fail*

By the time the song ended, Pierre had stopped crying. He shuffled toward them and patted Berlioz's head with a front paw.

"Thank you, kittens," he said, quickly patting Marie and Toulouse as well. "I needed that. Will you come visit me again?"

"Oh, most definitely," Marie said. "We come to the park all the time. . . ."

She froze and turned to her brothers. They all exchanged glances and at the same time cried, "Mama!"

"I'm so sorry, Pierre," Berlioz said. "Our mother and stepdad and human, they're all across the street getting ready for a picnic. If they realize we're not in the park—"

"They'll think we've been catnapped

again!" Marie finished the sentence for him. "But we'll be back soon, we promise!"

The kittens raced toward the door to the alley, climbing over one another to be the first to make it through.

# Chapter 3

Toulouse, Berlioz, and Marie all shared a cozy cat bed in the corner of Madame's room. It had supersoft blankets, silk pillows, and a curtain canopy. When the kittens didn't want to go to sleep, they stayed up and pretended their bed was a fort.

Not that night, though. Toulouse couldn't stop yawning, which made Berlioz yawn. Then those double yawns made Marie yawn, too.

"My darlings, you must be so tired from your adventure today," Duchess purred at them. She picked up Toulouse by the scruff of his neck and placed him gently under the covers.

"I've always wondered what happened to the Creature Café," O'Malley said as he nudged Berlioz with his nose until Berlioz crawled into his sleeping spot between Toulouse and Marie. "I ate there once, but it was too fancy for me. Not exactly my scene, you know? But plenty of my cat compadres liked to go for the sardine soup."

Marie snuggled in and sighed. "I really wish I could have seen it."

Duchess used her teeth to pull a blanket up to her kittens' chins. "Good night, darlings. May you all have sweet-cream dreams."

Duchess leaned over and kissed each kitten on the forehead. O'Malley gave them his most charming wink, and they winked back. Then the two big cats walked out of the room, leaving the door open a crack, because Berlioz was afraid of the dark.

Duchess was right: all three kittens really were exhausted. It took just a few

moments for them to fall fast asleep, purring—and, in Toulouse's case, snoring.

Marie's whiskers twitched as she started to dream. In her dream, the Creature Café was not a dusty, abandoned space but a busy cake and pastry shop—in France, they call this a pâtisserie—filled with many animal friends. There was Roquefort, the mouse, eating a slice of maple nut cheesecake. Somehow, Madame's horse, Frou Frou, was sitting at a table in the corner, wearing her flowered hat and declaring, "*Neeeeigh!* These are the best carrot apple cookies I've ever tasted!"

The dream version of Marie was in charge of the kitchen. She wore a chef's hat as she kneaded dough into kitty croissants like the ones her friend Louis made.

"Coming right up!" she murmured in her sleep.

On the opposite side of the bed, Toulouse was having his own amazing dream. The old restaurant had become an art gallery. Paintings created by Toulouse and other neighborhood creatures covered the bright white walls. Animals of all types wandered through the gallery, oohing and aahing over the art.

In between Toulouse and Marie, Berlioz started flicking his tail in his sleep. *Thwack-thwack-thwack.* The tapping made the beat to a song he played in his own dream, where he'd turned the café into a jazz club. His paws danced up and down the piano as cats from Alley Cat Parlor played their instruments along with him. Berlioz started singing.

Everyone in Berlioz's dream clapped and danced to his song. He was the jazz club's star, and a crowd of animals had gathered to see him perform. He raised his voice louder. . . .

The problem was, he wasn't just singing in his dream. He was singing in the real world, too. Toulouse jolted awake to the sound of Berlioz's musical stylings.

"Awww, man," Toulouse grumbled. "You and your sleep-yowling. I was in the middle of the best dream ever."

He flicked a paw at his brother's head. Berlioz's eyes popped open.

"Me too," Berlioz grumbled as he sat

up. "In *my* dream, I turned the old café into an awesome jazz club."

"A jazz club?" Toulouse echoed. "That's ridiculous. It's perfect for art, not music."

"But I need a place to perform!" Berlioz said, poking Toulouse.

"And I need somewhere to show my art!" Toulouse elbowed Berlioz.

Berlioz jumped on his brother.

"Music!" he growled as they started to wrestle, tumbling their way across the little bed.

"Art!" Toulouse growled back.

"No, music!"

"No, art!"

Toulouse tried to leap onto Berlioz but missed, landing on a still-snoozing Marie.

"Owwww!" she cried, opening her eyes. "What's happening?"

"Berlioz thinks the old café should be a silly jazz club," Toulouse told her.

"A jazz club would be better than a boring old art gallery," Berlioz said, rolling his eyes.

Marie stood up and huffed. "*Stop*! Both of you. Stop it right now. It's the middle of the night."

"Sorry . . ." the brothers mumbled.

"You should be," Marie said. "Especially because that *old* café should be turned into a *new* café. One where I'm the chef!"

Toulouse scrunched up his nose. "Eh. My idea's better."

"And mine is best of all," Berlioz added.

"You know there's only one way to settle this," Toulouse said, raising his eyebrows mischievously.

"Oh, no," Marie said with a sigh. "Not another Grand Staircase Race."

"First one to reach the bottom has the best idea. Ready? Set? Go!"

Before Marie could protest, Toulouse bounced out of bed, followed quickly by his brother. She leapt like lightning after them as all three scrambled through the open bedroom door toward the house's grand staircase. When they started to turn into the hallway, Berlioz caught up to Toulouse, grabbing at his tail to try to slow him down.

Toulouse let out a *"Mrrrrrow!"* and jumped out of reach, turning around for a second to stick out his tongue at

Berlioz. But he caught one claw on the rug and tripped over his own four feet.

Berlioz skidded to a stop. "Are you all right?" he asked his brother.

"I think so," Toulouse said, rubbing his face with one paw.

"See you guys later!" Marie shouted gleefully as she sped past them, around a corner, and toward the staircase.

"Come on," Berlioz said, pulling at Toulouse's blue bow collar with his teeth. "We can still catch her."

The brothers took off running again, their paws pitter-pattering. Berlioz reached the staircase first, but Marie was already halfway down.

"I can go faster than that," Berlioz said, and started hopping from step to step.

"That's fast," Toulouse called after him, "but taking stairs one at a time is for beginners!" Then Toulouse launched himself off the top of the staircase, flying over the first two steps and landing . . . right on Berlioz.

*"Mrrrrroooow!"* Berlioz squealed, toppling over. The two of them rolled down several steps and right into Marie, who had almost reached the bottom of the staircase.

Marie let out a startled *"Mee-oh!"* as all three kittens became one big ball of fur, tumbling down the final steps and onto the floor . . . toward a table holding a fancy china vase.

*BUMP.* They barreled right into one of the table legs. The china vase began to topple as the kittens broke apart and all shouted, "First!" at the same time.

The vase started falling. Berlioz, Marie, and Toulouse looked up in horror as they watched it sail through the air and . . .

In the blink of an eye, O'Malley jumped up, caught the vase with both paws, and landed on his back.

*THUD.*

The vase was safely hugged to Thomas's chest instead of shattered into a thousand pieces.

Duchess appeared and walked over to him. "Thomas, that was truly heroic! Are you all right?"

"Just dandy," O'Malley said. He sat up and carefully placed the vase next to him.

Duchess turned to her kittens and started thumping her tail hard against the floor. "Who is going to tell me why you're out of bed, chasing one another around in the dead of night, and almost breaking Madame's favorite vase?"

Toulouse stepped forward. "We had a good reason, I swear. It all started when each of us had a different dream about the old café."

Marie joined her brother. "I imagined it as a pâtisserie, Toulouse thinks it should be an art gallery, and Berlioz wants to make it his jazz club."

"So we tried to settle it with a race," Berlioz added. "Sorry, Mama. We've just been really bored. We want to do something new and fun."

Duchess took a long look at her

kittens. Then her blue eyes twinkled and she smiled. "You need another adventure, don't you?"

The kittens all nodded.

"My darlings," Duchess continued, "I know how you love to create and share what you create with others. I adore that about all three of you. But you each have something that's more important."

"Beautiful collars?" Marie asked.

"Sparkly toys?" Toulouse suggested.

"Sparkly toys *with bells inside?*" Berlioz guessed.

"You have one another," Duchess said.

Marie looked at Toulouse. Toulouse looked at Berlioz. Berlioz looked at a bug that had just started crawling up the wall.

"You are a team," Duchess said. "So

think as a team. Ask yourselves, *How can our ideas work together?*"

The kittens were quiet for a moment.

"Well," Marie began, "my pâtisserie would feel much cozier with art on the walls. . . ." She turned to Toulouse.

Toulouse's face lit up. "And great food and beautiful art go really well with . . ."

"Some hot jazz!" Berlioz exclaimed.

"A new café could have all three!" Marie declared.

"Now that is one lovely idea," Duchess said. "And you didn't need to shout and chase each other to decide on it, did you? Now, back to bed with you all. In the morning, you can figure out— *quietly*—what to do next."

The kittens glanced at one another. They already knew what to do next: they had to ask Pierre's permission to transform the old café. Hopefully, he'd say yes!

# Chapter 4

The next morning, three fuzzy streaks sped along the sidewalks of Paris—one white, one gray, and one orange. A human who looked closely would have seen a trio of kittens dashing as fast as they could toward their new bulldog friend. Toulouse, Berlioz, and Marie each wanted to be the first one to tell Pierre about their fantastic, fur-raising idea for the old café.

When they reached the corner of the

alley, they were all tied in the race. But
Toulouse leapt over Marie and took the
lead. He was so excited to be winning
one of their races, he turned back to
shout at his littermates.

"Haha! Slowpokes!"

*SPLASH.*

He ran right into a big puddle.

"*Me-EW!*" Toulouse cried, trying to
shake globs of mud off his face.

Marie and Berlioz skidded to a
stop, glanced at each other, and started
laughing.

"That's what you get," Berlioz
began, "when you—*Marieeeeeee!*"

While Berlioz was still chuckling,
Marie had dived toward the secret door.
She pawed at the tiny handle, but it
wouldn't open.

"Let me try," Toulouse said, swatting at Marie's head until she moved to give him room. But the handle didn't budge for him, either. "It must be locked."

Marie frowned, thinking. She took a few steps backward and stared up at the second-floor windows overlooking the alley. Pierre had told them he lived with his humans in an apartment above their restaurant. Maybe that was where he was now, and perhaps those were his windows.

"Pierre?" she shouted. "Pierre, are you home? It's Marie!"

"And Toulouse and Berlioz!" added Toulouse. "We need to talk to you!"

"What if we howled like the alley cats do?" Berlioz suggested. "That would catch his attention."

"Along with everyone else in the neighborhood," Toulouse said. "But you know me. I never say no to a howl."

All three kittens drew in a deep breath, then let loose with their loudest, longest howls. Their alley cat friends would have been proud! But the noises just echoed down the alley into silence.

Marie hung her head in disappointment. "He's not here."

"We'll have to try again tomorrow," Berlioz added.

"But I'm so excited!" Toulouse groaned. "We're *all* so excited! If I have to wait another day, I'll burst!"

"Well, try not to," Marie said, rolling her eyes.

The kittens shuffled out of the alley and back onto the street, headed toward home.

"Kittens!" A voice rang out above them. "Hi-hi-hi!"

Pouf, their squirrel friend, sat perched on a tree across the street, just inside the park fence.

Toulouse shouted up, "Hello, Pouf!"

"Are you here to play?" chattered the squirrel, flicking his bushy tail back and forth. "I'd like to play! We can play 'You-Chase-Me-up-a-Tree-but-I-Am-Always-Faster-than-You'!"

Toulouse started to reply: "Aw, we'd love to, but—"

"Hey!" Berlioz interrupted. "Have you seen our friend Pierre, the bulldog? He lives above that restaurant."

Pouf stared at them for a few long moments, twitching his nose.

"Pierre, the Dog-Who-Thinks-He-Can-Catch-Me-but-Never-Can?"

"Ummm," Marie said. "Probably?"

"Pierre, who used to run the Creature Café?" Pouf added.

"Yes!" Marie exclaimed. "You know the café?"

"Every animal who lived in the park

back then knows about it. They served the *best* berry acorn tarts! Yum-yum-yummy-yum!"

"We have an idea to start up the café again," Toulouse shouted up. "We're looking for Pierre so we can get his permission."

"Café? Again? More YUM?" Pouf babbled. The kittens nodded. "Follow me! I think I know where you can find him!"

Pouf scrambled down from the tree as the kittens darted across the street and through the park fence. Duchess would never let them enter the park that way instead of through the front gate. But the kittens were definitely not thinking about what was proper and what wasn't. They'd learned that sometimes, in order to tackle a big task, you had to try something new.

When they caught up with Pouf, the squirrel said, "I saw him earlier at the pond. Come on!"

Now there were four fuzzy streaks, bouncing and barreling down the Luxembourg Gardens paths toward the water basin, where dogs often liked to bring their humans.

But when they reached the basin, there was no sign of Pierre.

"Pierre!" Toulouse shouted. "Pierre?"

A voice came from the pond: "Is your friend a French bulldog?" One of the ducks paddled in place, watching them.

"Yes!" Marie replied. "Have you seen him?"

"Just a few minutes ago," the duck said. "He picked up a strange dog's scent and started following it. I think he was headed for the fountain."

"I know a supersecret squirrel shortcut!" babbled Pouf. "This way!"

The fuzzy streaks were off again, through some bushes and across rocks. Duchess *definitely* would have disapproved. When they reached the park's big stone fountain, the kittens scanned the area, huffing and puffing from their run.

"There!" Berlioz exclaimed, pointing a paw.

Pierre was sniffing his way down a path, wagging his tail in excitement.

Now the race to reach Pierre first was on again. The kittens tumbled and tangled with one another as they ran, but Toulouse grabbed the lead. When he reached Pierre, he stopped short. Marie got there next, but when she stopped, she stumbled over Toulouse. When Berlioz saw that, he tried to leap over them both . . . but landed right on Pierre's back.

"Ouch!" Pierre barked.

"I'm so sorry!" Berlioz sputtered. "And also . . . hello."

"Pierre," Marie said, "we really need to talk to you!"

"Bah! I was on the trail of the most interesting-smelling dog." Pierre sighed and gave the kittens an annoyed look. "This had better be important."

Toulouse, Marie, and Berlioz began speaking at the same time.

"We want to open a new café—"

"There will be food and music and art—"

"We'll run it, but we need your help stocking the kitchen—"

"*ROWWWWWWFFF.*" Pierre let out a long, gruff bark.

The kittens got the hint and quieted down. Berlioz hopped off Pierre's back and joined his littermates.

"Let me get this straight," Pierre said. "You want to reopen the old Creature Café?"

"Serving up sweet and savory treats," Marie said.

"With jazz music," Berlioz added.

"And amazing art on the walls," Toulouse chimed in.

"This will be run by . . . the three of you?" Pierre asked.

"Yes," Marie said, "working as a *team*. Right, boys?"

Toulouse and Berlioz nodded.

"Mama says we can do more together than we can apart," Marie said.

Pierre thought about that. "Your mama sounds very smart. But I'm not sure. It won't be easy to get that old café fixed up. The furniture needs to be repaired and painted. There are plates and cups and baking pans tossed here and there. You'd have to find them all and wash, then polish them. It will all take so much time."

"We have time," Toulouse said. "Lots and lots of time!"

"And energy, too, I'm sure," Pierre said with a smile. "But what about the food? Where will that come from?"

"Um, well . . ." Berlioz began. "We were hoping you could get it from the restaurant upstairs, like you did for Monsieur Midnight."

"Just like the old days, Pierre!" Pouf exclaimed from his perch on a rock. "Yum-yum-yummy-yum!"

"Ah, yes," Pierre said dreamily, a smile growing on his face. "Just like the old days with my friend Midnight . . ."

Marie, Toulouse, and Berlioz all exchanged glances. Was Pierre going to give the paws-up?

But Pierre sighed. "I'm sorry, children, but no . . . As much as I'd love to reopen the café, I just don't see it. You have no idea how much work it takes to run a café."

Toulouse and Berlioz let their tails

drop and their ears droop. They were filled with disappointment. Not Marie, though. She stood up even straighter.

"Let us see for ourselves," she said.

"*Pardon?*" Pierre asked.

"Let us see for ourselves how much work it is! We could do a kind of tryout. I'll create a sample menu. Berlioz, you can play some of your music. And Toulouse can paint a huge mural to decorate one of those dirty, dusty walls."

"We would need some customers for the tryout, too," Toulouse said.

"Who do we know who would want to sample your cooking, Marie?" Berlioz asked.

The kittens all looked at one another and had the same idea at the exact same time.

"Roquefort!" they exclaimed together.

"Let me guess," Pierre said. "With a cheese name like that, Roquefort is a mouse?"

"One of our best friends," Toulouse said. "He's always up for helping us."

"Plus, he knows a lot of other hungry mice," Berlioz added.

Pierre gazed at Berlioz, then at Toulouse, and finally at Marie. Had they done enough to convince him?

"You are three *very* determined kittens," Pierre said, sighing. "If you can put all that determination into the café, it will really be something."

"Does that mean yes?" Marie asked.

Pierre broke into a huge grin and nodded. "Let's give it a try."

Marie cheered, "Yay! Oh, thank you, thank you, Monsieur Pierre. You won't regret this! Berlioz, you run home and ask Roquefort if he can be our tryout guest. Toulouse, can you go with him and collect your paint supplies? You'll need to get started on the mural right away."

"We're on it!" the brothers both shouted over their shoulders as they scurried away.

"Oh," Pierre said, watching them go. "So you meant . . . you were going to do all this *right now*."

"Now I need to plan a little menu," Marie said, pacing back and forth across the park path. "Pierre, can we get ingredients from the restaurant?"

Pierre thought for a moment. "We'll

have to sneak into the kitchen before the lunch rush, but that should be easy. I used to do it all the time."

"We also need to find those dishes and baking supplies," Marie reminded him.

"I think I remember where they are," Pierre said.

"Can I help, too? Can I help, too?" squeaked Pouf from the rock.

Marie watched Pouf's huge fluffy tail swish back and forth, back and forth. Then she got an idea.

"The café floor is really dirty," Marie told him. "Could you sweep it for us?"

Pouf twitched his nose a few times before agreeing. "Sure! Okay! Yes! No problem!"

He scrambled off the rock and disappeared into a bush.

"If we're going to get ingredients from the restaurant," Pierre said, "we'll have to hurry."

Marie followed Pierre out of the park and across the street to the Luxembourg Brasserie. He scratched at a front window while Marie hid under a chair at one of the outdoor tables. A human came and opened the door.

"Out exploring again, Pierre?" the human asked him. Pierre let out a soft bark as he trotted into the restaurant. When the waiter was looking the other way, Marie slipped in behind Pierre.

But she accidentally brushed her tail against the human's leg.

# Chapter 5

"**H**uh?" the waiter said, glancing down.

Marie moved like lightning to hide behind Pierre. The waiter couldn't see her, so he shrugged and closed the front door, then walked away.

"Bah!" Pierre said. "That was a close one."

"I guess sometimes being little is a *good* thing," Marie added.

"Follow me. The restaurant kitchen is over there."

It wasn't long before Marie and Pierre were climbing down the restaurant's back stairs to the old Creature Café. Each carried a basket filled with berries, nuts, cream, flour, butter, eggs, and more.

When Marie saw what the café looked like now, she almost dropped her basket. The floors were already sparkling clean!

Pouf sat on a windowsill, brushing his tail. "Did I do a good job? Did I? Yes? Yes?"

"Good?" Marie laughed. "Pouf, you did an *amazing* job! How can I ever thank you?"

"Three words: Acorn. Berry. Tart. Acorn berry tart! Remember that!"

As he dashed out the door to the alley, Marie shouted after him, "You got it!"

Toulouse and Berlioz returned, and there was no time to waste. Roquefort happily agreed to act as the customer for their tryout and would be there soon, along with some hungry mouse friends.

Marie popped a tray of cheddar walnut puffs into the oven. They didn't look exactly like the ones she'd once cooked with Louis, but she hoped they tasted just as good. Berlioz rehearsed on the old piano while Toulouse worked on his mural. As Marie started to wash some old plates she'd found in the kitchen, Berlioz's voice rang out through the café. He sang about scales and arpeggios.

*"Urrrrr!"* Marie grumbled. "It sounds like that piano *hates* the scales and arpeggios. We're lucky Mama isn't here."

"Well, it's not my fault," Berlioz replied. "I tried to tune it, but it didn't help."

"Could you at least stop playing until we find someone to fix it? It's really distracting!"

"Toulouse doesn't seem distracted." Berlioz pointed at their brother, who was scooping up green paint from a can with his paws.

"You know how he gets when he's

doing art," Marie said. "He doesn't pay attention to anything else."

They both watched Toulouse for a moment. He smeared a blob of the green paint on the wall next to a blob of pink paint.

"Hey, Toulouse!" Berlioz said, moving closer. "What exactly are you painting, anyway? I thought you were going to make it look like a window with a view of the park."

Toulouse glared at his brother. "Ahem, that *is* what I'm painting."

"Really?" Marie asked. "Because it looks like you just splattered colors all over the place."

"It's modern art," Toulouse said, "and it's better than your music on that broken piano!"

The brothers scowled at each other as Marie looked over the rest of the wall. At the very top of the mural, big letters spelled out THE PAINT PALETTE PÂTISSERIE.

"And what's that?" Marie asked Toulouse, pointing to the letters.

"That's what I think we should name the café. Do you like it?"

"But this isn't a café about painting!" Berlioz protested. "Plus, I have a much better idea for the name: the Jazz-a-ma-tazz Pâtisserie."

Marie and Toulouse exchanged glances.

"That's too hard to say," Marie said. "And we might want to play other music besides just jazz."

"Let me guess," Berlioz said. "You've come up with the perfect name."

"Well . . ." Marie began, smiling. "This is a critter café, right? And the food will be tasty. So I was thinking we should name it the Tasty Tails Pâtisserie."

"Ew," Toulouse said. "It sounds like we're baking tails into the food!"

The brothers laughed while Marie sat there, thinking. "Okay, that does sound a little strange. But you don't have to tease me about it."

Suddenly, Berlioz stopped giggling and sat up straight. "Hey, do you smell something burning?" he asked.

Marie sniffed the air. "My puffs!" she cried, darting into the kitchen.

When she opened the oven, a cloud of gray smoke billowed out. Marie removed the tray and dropped it on the counter. One of the puffs had caught fire! She blew on it like a birthday candle until the flame went out. But the other puffs were completely black and burnt on the bottom.

Marie sat down on the kitchen floor, tears welling up in her eyes.

"Maybe Pierre was right," she said, sniffling. "Maybe it's just too hard to run a café. Especially for us. We can't do anything without ending up in a fight."

Berlioz's tail drooped, and Toulouse shuffled his paws against the floor. The brothers exchanged guilty looks. They both went to their sister.

Berlioz gave Marie a quick, comforting lick on her nose. "I'm sorry I made fun of your name idea."

"And I'm sorry your puffs got burned," Toulouse added, nuzzling her. "I'll paint a better mural, and Berlioz will get that piano fixed. Won't you, Berlioz?"

Berlioz nodded and said, "Don't give up yet, Marie. I know we can make this happen."

Marie wiped away her tears with one

paw and looked at her brothers. "Hey, you both said sorry without Mama here to remind you. Maybe we *can* work as a team."

"Maybe we just need some helping paws," Toulouse suggested.

Marie suddenly sat up straight. "Yes, we do! And I know exactly who to ask!"

# Chapter 6

"I need to go home," Marie said.

"Why?" Berlioz asked, confused.

"Home is where Alley Cat Parlor is," Marie continued. "And Alley Cat Parlor is where Louis is. Louis is a chef, get it? He can help me with the menu!"

"Great idea, Marie!" Toulouse exclaimed. "We'll go with you if you'd like. Teams should stick together."

Marie thought for a moment. "Right now, I think teamwork means that you keep working on the mural, and, Berlioz, you keep trying to fix the piano. That way we'll get three things done at once."

"I like the sound of that," Berlioz said, and Toulouse nodded in agreement.

"I'll be back as soon as I can," Marie told them.

She darted out the secret door and raced home, imagining all the scrumptious café treats Louis could help her make. Once she arrived at Madame's, she ran straight through the kitty door, past the grand staircase, and down the main hallway, then pushed open the big wooden door to Alley Cat Parlor.

She found Louis curled up on a purple velvet cushion by the fireplace.

He was fast asleep, his paws and whiskers twitching.

"Louis," Marie whispered. When he didn't wake up, she said his name a bit louder. "Louis!"

One eye blinked open, then the other. "Are you okay, Mademoiselle Marie?" Louis said as he raised his head. "You're out of breath."

Marie's words tumbled out quickly. "I ran all the way here from . . . Well, this is the first thing I need to tell you: my brothers and I want to open up our own café for the animals of Paris! We'd serve kitty croissants and cheddar walnut puffs and salmon mousse and all the other treats you've taught me how to make."

"Ah, Marie," Louis said, his eyes shining. "That sounds wonderful."

"But first we need to pull off a tryout to prove we can do it. And I know we can. It's just that . . . well, we could use an extra set of paws and, of course, your expertise as a chef. Monsieur Louis, would you please help us?"

"Help you cook and bake for a café?" Louis paused, thinking. "I haven't done anything like that in years. Perhaps it's time."

"Oh, thank you, Louis!" Marie

exclaimed, hugging him. "And just wait until you meet Pierre!"

Louis narrowed his eyes. "Pierre?"

"Our new friend. The café is in the secret basement of Pierre's humans' restaurant, the Luxembourg Brasserie. Near the park. It used to be called Le Café des Crea—"

Louis held up a paw, signaling Marie to stop. "I'm sorry. I was mistaken. I can't help after all."

"What?"

"I just remembered that—you see, I'm very busy—unfortunately I have somewhere to be right now and I'm already late."

With that, Louis fled from the room in a flash of black fur.

Marie blinked at the spot where

Louis had been sitting. "What just happened?"

Had she offended Louis? Where could he be rushing to? Why would he say he could help, then change his mind so quickly? And what should she do now? If Marie and her brothers failed the tryout, Pierre wouldn't let them open the café.

She had to think. Marie slunk out of Alley Cat Parlor and went to the one place she knew she could be alone with her thoughts: a special spot that nobody else knew about.

Marie crept into Madame's private study, then quietly jumped onto an open drawer, then a stack of books, then the back of a chair, and finally the top of the bookcase by the window. She lay down with her head on her paws, closing her eyes to the sun streaming in from outside.

She thought of her dream, where she was serving up treats to animal friends in a busy, happy pâtisserie. Then she added to that image, with Berlioz's music filling the air and Toulouse's art brightening the walls. All three kittens were cheerful and proud of their work as a team.

*WHOMP!*

Something furry and heavy landed on her. Marie opened her eyes to see Toulouse, smiling wide.

"Looks like we finally found your hideout," he said.

"I'll get you back the next time *you're* having a great nap," Marie said with a laugh as she swatted at Toulouse's bow.

"What did Louis say?" Berlioz called

from below. "Will he help us? And what are you doing up there when there's so much work to do at the café?"

Marie peered down at her brother. A small cloth bag lay at his feet.

"Why aren't *you* at the café?" she asked.

"We found something very interesting. Come down and see."

Marie sighed as she stood up and made her way to down to her brother. Toulouse followed.

"It's a bunch of photographs from the Creature Café," Berlioz said as his littermates landed softly on the floor. He nudged the bag toward Marie. "I discovered them in a box that was stuck inside the piano. That's what was making it sound so awful."

Berlioz opened the bag, and dozens of photos tumbled out. In them, all types of animals posed at the café tables: mice and rats and rabbits. Chipmunks and squirrels and groundhogs. Pigeons and ducks and geese. Dogs and cats and— wow!—even a pig.

"They all look like they're having so much fun," Marie said wistfully. "I'm

glad you found this, Berlioz. It really gives me inspiration to make the café work somehow."

"Hey," Toulouse said, pointing with his paw to one particular photo. "There's Pierre."

Marie leaned in to get a better look. In the picture, Pierre stood under a sign that said WELCOME TO LE CAFÉ DES CREATURES.

Next to him stood a fluffy black cat—who looked *very* familiar.

"It's Louis!" Marie cried. "They know each other! Now that I think of it, Louis changed his mind about helping us as soon as I said Pierre's name. . . ."

Berlioz pointed to another photo. In this one, Louis was in the kitchen on his

hind legs, holding out a tray of kitty croissants.

"Mmm," Toulouse said. "Looking at these photos is making me hungry."

"What does his chef's hat say?" Berlioz asked.

Marie leaned in close so she could read the writing on the hat.

"Oh. Meow. Gosh!" she said. "It says 'Monsieur Midnight'! Louis is Monsieur Midnight!"

"Yes," said someone behind them. "I'm Monsieur Midnight."

# Chapter 7

"Louis!" Marie exclaimed.

The fluffy black cat sat in the doorway of Madame's study with a chef's hat on the floor in front of him.

"I'm sorry I ran off like that," he said. "I was just so surprised to hear you mention Pierre and Le Café des Creatures. And, you know, we are cats, after all. Cats *hate* surprises."

"I'm confused," Berlioz said. "Pierre

told us that Monsieur Midnight and his human moved to America."

"Yes, that was the plan," Louis said. "But right before we were supposed to leave, I realized I would miss my beloved Paris too much. My human could tell I didn't want to move, so he let me stay behind. I've always wanted to live the alley cat life! I'm happy, but I wish I could see my old friend Pierre."

"Then why didn't you go tell him you were still here?" Toulouse asked.

Louis hung his head. "Pierre is a very loyal dog. At first I was afraid he'd still be angry with me, because *his* human was angry with *my* human, and we had such an awful fight. Then the more time passed, the harder it became to go visit him."

"Oh, Louis . . ." Marie said. "I think Pierre misses you very much, too. You should have seen his face when he talked about Monsieur Midnight and all the fun you two had running the café."

"He remembers all the fun?" Louis asked, his face brightening.

"Yes!" Marie said. "And obviously, so do you. We *have* to get you back together."

Louis waved his paw. "Don't worry about that. We have a café tryout to plan."

"But first we have a friendship to save," Marie said.

"That's more important," Berlioz
added.

Toulouse thought quietly for a few
moments. Then he exclaimed, "Hey,
I think I have a plan for both those
things!"

Late afternoon light seeped in through
the small windows of the café, throwing
patterns across the floor. Toulouse
worked on his mural while Berlioz
repaired a broken table leg with a piece
of chewing gum he'd found in the alley.

He paused, sniffed the air, and
turned to his brother. "Mmmm," he
murmured. "Fresh cream."

Toulouse nodded. "Cheese, too. And
spinach. Also, maybe a tomato?"

"Plus eggs. They must be making quiche!"

Both brothers began to purr at the delicious thought.

In the kitchen, Marie peeked into the oven. Louis had fixed it, but she was still worried about another food-on-fire situation. The black cat stood near the counter, mixing up cookie batter for dessert.

*Knock-knock.*

"Hello?" a squeaky voice called from outside the secret café door. "Kittens, are you here?"

"It's Roquefort!" Berlioz told Toulouse. "Go let him in!"

Toulouse opened the door to find their mouse friend, dressed up in a little red cap and coat.

"Greetings, Berlioz!" Roquefort said, and stepped aside to reveal three other mice, also wearing coats. "This is my cousin Brie, and my other cousin, Camembert, and my *other* other cousin, Munster."

"Welcome to our café!" Toulouse said, leading them inside to a mouse-sized table. "I'll take your coats."

"Your meal should be ready soon," said Berlioz. "I can play you a song while you're waiting."

Berlioz sat down at the piano and started to play one of his new jazz tunes. The instrument sounded much better now that it didn't have a box of old photos buried inside it.

Pierre appeared on the back stairs.

"Is it time yet?" he called. "It smells like it might be."

"Yes," Toulouse told him, pointing to a dog-sized table set with a matching plate, cup, and silverware. "We set this table just for you."

"Psssst," Marie whispered to her brothers from the kitchen doorway. "Come here. Your bows are crooked."

Berlioz and Toulouse let their sister fix the ribbons around their necks.

"There," Marie said when she was done. "Now, here's a cart with the quiche and lemonade. Don't you dare drop anything!"

"Sure, Mademoiselle Chef," Berlioz said. He wheeled the cart to Roquefort,

his cousins, and Pierre. He and Toulouse had barely finished passing out all the food and drinks when Roquefort declared, "Dee-li-ci-ous! Double dee-li-ci-ous, in fact!"

The mice were gobbling up the quiche, but Pierre was taking his time. He scooped up one pawful, popped it in his mouth, and chewed slowly.

"Bah!" Pierre said. "This tastes so much like Monsieur Midnight's quiche it's eerie. It brings back many memories."

"Good memories?" Berlioz asked.

"Definitely," Pierre said with a smile. "Although I must say, this quiche might even be better than his. His quiche was always a little too . . . cheesy."

"TOO CHEESY?" someone howled

from the kitchen. "You were always telling me to put *more* cheese in it!"

Pierre froze midchew, then swallowed hard. He slowly turned toward the voice. When he saw Louis standing in the kitchen doorway, his mouth fell open.

"M-M-Midnight?" he stammered.

Berlioz and Toulouse slunk into the kitchen to join Marie, and the three kittens crouched down to watch what happened next.

"Hello, mon ami," Louis said, taking a few steps forward. "It's good to see your face."

"Wh-wh-what are you doing here?" Pierre asked.

"I'm here to help my friends Berlioz, Toulouse, and Marie learn how to run a café. The animals of Paris need to have their own eatery again, don't you think?"

Pierre hopped off his chair and stepped closer to Louis so their noses were nearly touching.

"I thought you were in America," Pierre said.

"I thought you never wanted to speak to me again," Louis said in return. "That was quite a fight we had that day my human told yours he was leaving."

"It was," Pierre said with a nod. "But we shouldn't have let one fight ruin a whole friendship."

"I agree." Louis bowed his head. "Is it too late to say I'm sorry?"

"Not for me," Pierre replied. "I'm

sorry, too, my friend. Bah, how I've missed you!"

They touched noses. The kittens exchanged excited glances. Success!

"My quiche *was* too cheesy back then, wasn't it?" Louis added. "I've learned not to use so much."

The brown-and-white bulldog and the fluffy black cat laughed.

After a few moments, Toulouse bounded toward them and said, "Hey, Pierre? How did we do on our tryout? Do you think we can run a café?"

Pierre smiled. "Bah! I certainly do! Maybe you can talk Monsieur Midnight into coming in to help again."

The kittens started jumping on one another in excitement. "Yay! Woo-hoo!"

"But I can't officially say yes," Pierre

added, "unless you agree to one more thing."

Marie, Berlioz, and Toulouse stopped wrestling. *One more thing?*

"The name of the café," Pierre continued. "It came to me in a dream last night."

He held up a paw to Toulouse's mural, showing them where the words might appear. "The Purrfect Paw-tisserie."

Everyone fell silent for a moment.

"I love it!" Berlioz exclaimed.

"Ha ha ha!" Toulouse laughed. "Yes!"

"That's the best name ever," Marie said, rushing to nuzzle the bulldog. "Thank you, Monsieur Pierre! Thank you!"

"Together, we all make a great team," Louis said.

Berlioz thought for a moment, then chimed in: "Everything does come out better when we get over our differences and cooperate."

"Yes," Pierre agreed. "And that's good . . . because we still have lots of work to do."

# Chapter 8

Welcome, friends furry, scaly &
feathery!

Enjoy life at the purrfect
paw-tisserie!

High up on a ladder, Toulouse
finished the final *E* on the café's new
slogan. The letters were bright gold, and
below them, he'd filled his park painting
with greens for the leaves and grass,
brown for the walkways, and blue for
the sky.

It was opening day at the brand-new café.

"The more I stare at it, the more I see what a lovely park it is," Marie said, standing next to a cart full of fresh-baked dog bone biscuits and looking over the mural. "Your art is really beautiful, Toulouse."

"The other walls look cool, too," Berlioz said from his bench at the piano. He glanced up at the wall above him, where Toulouse had hung several framed paintings by other neighborhood cats. One was a portrait of a fish, called *I Love Tuna!* Another was a view of Paris rooftops at night, surrounded by stars, with the simple title of *Home.*

"When do we get to hear your new

song?" Marie asked Berlioz, pushing her tray of biscuits into a big glass pastry case. The cats from Alley Cat Parlor had built it for them. Inside were rows and rows of colorful treats.

"I'm not going to play it until the grand opening party," Berlioz replied. "So you'll just have to wait."

Marie stuck out her tongue at Berlioz. Berlioz gave her a *fffffft* in

return. Then they both giggled and grinned at each other.

"Enough of that, my darlings," called their mother. Duchess and O'Malley had come in while the kittens were busy with their last-minute tasks.

"Mama!" Berlioz squealed, spinning on his piano stool with his arms out wide. "What do you think?"

Duchess walked slowly around the café, swishing among the freshly painted white tables of all different animal sizes. O'Malley leaned in to the pastry case and sniffed, his whiskers and ears twitching.

"App-e-ti-zing, baby!" he said.

"It's lovely from top to bottom," Duchess declared. "I'm so proud of you, children!"

"Thank you, Mama!" the kittens cried, rushing to nuzzle her.

Pierre and Louis came in through the secret door. When Pierre saw Duchess and the kittens, he said, "I hate to break up this giant cat cuddle, but you have some hungry guests outside, waiting to come in."

"Just one more moment, if you please, Monsieur Pierre," Duchess said to him, then turned back to her kittens. "Working together to get the café ready was not always easy for you . . . but you did it! This is such a special day. Can you get through it without any more fighting?"

"Of course we can, Mama!" Marie said, then blinked her long lashes a few times. "Or at least, I know *I* can."

"Me too," Toulouse added.

"Me *three*," Berlioz insisted.

"We do argue a little," Marie admitted. "Or maybe *a lot*. But we really do make a great team."

"Very well, then," Duchess said with a smile. "Pierre and Louis, please open the door!"

Pierre and Louis smiled at each other, and together, the two old friends threw open the secret door in the grate and said: "*Bonjour!* The Purrfect Paw-tisserie welcomes you!"

Four sets of scurrying little feet—belonging to Roquefort and his cousins Brie, Camembert, and Munster—rushed inside and up to the pastry case.

"Hello, kittens!" Roquefort greeted them. "We couldn't wait to come back and try more of your—Good heavens! Look at all these treats!"

As the mice began picking out items from the pastry case, something moved like a streak across the floor.

"Pardon me! Pardon me! Acorn-berry-tart-pardon-me!"

Pouf skittered toward one of the squirrel-sized tables, picked up the chair, and started chewing on it.

"Pouf, no!" Toulouse cried. "The treats are over there! Behind the glass!"

Marie handed him a tart, which he popped in his mouth whole and stored in his cheek. "So good! So good! Yum-yum-yum-can-I-have-another!"

The door opened again.

"Louis!" half a dozen cats from the Alley Cat Parlor sang as they rushed in.

Suddenly, the Purrfect Paw-tisserie swirled with activity. Marie and Louis served up treats while several of the alley cats gathered around the piano, singing along with Berlioz as he played a song about how wonderful it was to be a cat. Roquefort and his cousins tasted every single type of treat in the pastry case while O'Malley and Duchess admired Toulouse's artwork.

After a little while, Pierre went to the piano and barked to get everyone's attention. The crowd quieted down and gathered around.

"I think I speak for both myself and my dear old friend Monsieur Louis Midnight," Pierre began, "when I say it's wonderful to once again see the animals of Paris gathered here. I had my doubts

that it would work, but Berlioz, Toulouse, and Marie have shown us what they can do with some kitten creativity and collaboration. Congratulations, you three!"

Everyone applauded. Marie took a step forward. Toulouse took two steps forward. Both of them stopped when Berlioz hopped on top of his piano stool.

"Thank you!" Berlioz said, taking a bow. "You know, the night I had a dream we opened our own café, it looked a lot like this, and then—"

"Ah, so this was all *your* idea!" Brie the mouse exclaimed. "You deserve a special round of applause!"

Before Berlioz could correct her, everyone started clapping again. Marie and Toulouse exchanged confused glances.

The crowd cheered: "HOORAY, BERLIOZ! BRAVO! BRAVO!"

"Oh!" Berlioz said, realizing what he'd done. "No, wait!" But nobody heard him above the noise. "Hello? Everyone?"

He spun around and banged his paws on the piano keys. The whole café fell silent.

"I think there has been a misunderstanding," Berlioz announced, then spotted Marie and Toulouse in the crowd. "This wasn't just my idea. My brother and sister and I . . . well, we did it all together. Marie? Toulouse? Will you come sit with me at the piano?"

Toulouse and Marie smiled and

made their way, purring, up to the top of the piano.

"You see . . ." Berlioz continued. "Well . . . let me tell you the story the best way I know how."

One by one, he stretched out all ten toes on his front paws, then all eight on his back paws, making a big cracking noise each time. Finally, he started playing and singing:

*We're just three little kittens, but*
*wait, you should listen*
*To the story of this here café*
*We have paws and tails and*
*whiskers, then we start to differ*
*We each spend time our own way*
*Toulouse paints the world, with colors*
*swished and swirled*

*To brighten your walls and your day*
*Marie mixes and measures, bakes fun*
*into treasures*
*"Can I please have some more?" they*
*all say*
*As for me, I do my part by singing*
*what's in my heart*
*Just give me some cool jazz to play*
*We kittens worked together to bring*
*YOU all together*
*And now that you're here, we'll let*
*out a cheer*
*For food and art and song*
*And everyone getting along*
*At the Purrfect Paw-tisserie!*

When the song ended, everyone
applauded even more loudly than before.

Duchess beamed with pride at her kittens. Marie and Toulouse leapt off the piano and into the air toward their brother . . . landing on him in a triple-kitten cuddle. They cuddled for a long time, purring together.

After a few minutes, Louis came up and tapped Marie on the shoulder.

"Ahem, Marie? I'm sorry to tell you this, but I think you have another problem."

"Problem? What is it?" Marie asked.

"Come with me," Louis said, his face serious. "I'll show you."

Marie, Toulouse, and Berlioz exchanged worried expressions. What could be the matter *now*?

He led the kittens to one of the windows overlooking the alley. They had to climb a chair, then hop onto the frame of a painting and onto the windowsill.

Out in the alley, there were animals. Lots of animals! More cats and dogs, hamsters and rabbits, and so many squirrels it was hard to tell where one ended and another began.

"What are they doing?" Berlioz asked.

"What do you think?" Louis said. "They're waiting to get into the café! News travels fast among the animals of Paris. Oh, my, you're going to be busy. Can you handle it?"

Marie, Berlioz, and Toulouse

exchanged smiles. It was like a secret language between them now. The smile said: *Together, we can do anything.*

Marie said, "Open the door, Louis. We're ready!"

**Jennifer Castle** is the author of over a dozen books for kids and teens, including the Butterfly Wishes series and American Girl's Girl of the Year: Blaire books. She lives in New Paltz, New York, with her family, which includes five cats, a leopard gecko, and, often, a few rescued foster kittens, who are all likely planning their own creature café when the humans aren't looking.

**Sydney Hanson** is a children's book illustrator living in Sierra Madre, California. Her illustrations reflect her growing up with numerous pets and brothers in Minnesota, and her love of animals and nature. She illustrates using both traditional and digital media; her favorites are watercolor and colored pencil. When she's not drawing, she enjoys running, baking, and exploring the woods with her family. To see her latest animals and illustrations, follow her on Instagram at @sydwiki.